THANKS FOR

Aggie didn't have any aunties worth mentioning. Actually she did have two, but they weren't what you'd call REAL aunties, not in the strict sense of the word. Put it this way; in the cheek-chukkering, cake-making, trip-taking stakes, they were non-starters. In fact, I would go so far as to say that if you were to take two cauliflowers, place them on the top of two swing bins and sellotape the word AUNTY to each of them, they would make better aunties than the ones Aggie had.

THANKS FOR THE SARDINE

Written and illustrated by
LAURA BEAUMONT

RED FOX

For My Mum

*Oh, yes . . . and special thanks to Dolly and the Nipper –
without whose supremely useless visit, this book
would never have been written.*

"I've got a Lovely Bunch of Coconuts" © 1944 and
1948 by the Urwin Dash Music Co. Ltd.
Reprinted by kind permission of
Box & Cox Publications Ltd.

A Red Fox Book

Published by Random House Children's Books
20 Vauxhall Bridge Road, London SW1V 2SA

A division of Random House UK Ltd
London Melbourne Sydney Auckland
Johannesburg and agencies throughout the world

First published by The Bodley Head 1991

Red Fox edition 1992

Text and illustrations copyright © Laura Beaumont 1991

Phototypeset in Plantin by Intype, London
Printed and bound in Great Britain by
Cox & Wyman Ltd, Reading, Berkshire

ISBN 0 09 997900 4

CHAPTER ONE

Sardines & Sundays

This is a story about Aggie. Well, actually, it's not JUST about Aggie, it's about lots of other people as well, but we won't be meeting them until later. Anyway, back to Aggie.

Aggie was a very cheerful girl. Everybody said so.

Except on Mondays. Aggie was never cheerful on Mondays.

Monday was the day when all Aggie's friends came into school brimming with marvellously exciting stories about what they'd done on Sunday with their AUNTIES. And that's not all!

Some of them would have lovely round, full tummies from having been fed a mountain of cream cakes. Some would even have smart red *chukkering* marks on their cheeks. For those of you who don't know what a *chukkering* mark is, let me explain.

It's a little red mark that's left after an aunty (and it's usually only aunties who do this) grabs your cheek between thumb and forefinger and waggles it about.

Chukker
Chukker

While they are doing this they are usually saying something like this: "Who's a lovely chubby chops den?"

It's a sign of affection. Try it and see!

Anyway; Aggie always listened sadly to her friends' stories. Never once, had she come in on a Monday with a smart red mark on her cheek or a lovely full tummy or indeed been able to

3

recount an exciting tale about what she'd got up to on Sunday. The reason for this, if you haven't already guessed it, was: Aggie didn't have any aunties. Well, – none worth mentioning. Actually she did have two, but they weren't what you'd call REAL aunties, not in the strict sense of the word. Put it this way; in the cheek-chukkering, cake-making, trip-taking stakes, they were non-starters. In fact, I would go so far as to say that if you were to take two cauliflowers, place them on the top of two swing bins and sellotape the word AUNTY to each of them, they would make better aunties than the ones Aggie had.

It wasn't that they meant to be useless aunties, bless their old hearts, it was just that they weren't very good at it; like some people aren't very good at swimming or playing tennis. THEY weren't very good at being aunties. (Actually they weren't very good at swimming or playing tennis either but that's another story.)

So it wasn't any wonder that Aggie was a bit sad on a Monday.

But what of these two useless specimens of auntihood? I hear you ask. Well, allow me to introduce them to you. Their names are Aunty Prin and Aunty Min and they look like this:

Useless, eh?

But let's not judge a book by its cover. To prove my point I will show you a picture of the winner of this year's "Funniest Uncle Award".

This man has been known to balance a small child on his head, waggle his ears, make his thumb appear and disappear, pretend to take away several children's noses, make a glove puppet out of a sock, AND whistle *Old McDonald had a Farm* . . .

ALL AT THE SAME TIME!

Although you certainly
wouldn't expect it,
from the look of him.

So let's find out a bit more about Aggie's aunties. Well, for start-offs, they lived in the most boring house that you could possibly imagine.

Are you imagining? Does what you're imagining look like this?

WELL, IT'S NOT BORING ENOUGH!
IMAGINE HARDER!

O.K. I'll give you a clue.

Their house was so boring it made the sort of house small children draw look interesting.

The sort of house small children draw.

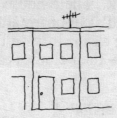

The useless aunties' house.

See what I mean! And the inside was almost as boring as the outside.

There were no frilly curtains at the windows, no lacy covers on the chairs, no rows of old photographs in shiny silver frames, no fat, purring old moggy by the fireside. And worst of all . . . NO KNICK-KNACKS!

Now for the benefit of those of you who don't know what a knick-knack is, let me explain.

A knick-knack is a small, decorative and completely useless object. Here is a small selection:

Proper aunties always have knick-knacks, loads of them, all over the place, each with a tale to tell and a smell that lurks somewhere between damp cardboard and dusty muffins.

7

But Aunty Prin and Aunty Min had neither knick nor knack. Their house was as bare as Mother Hubbard's cupboard after a particularly thorough spring clean. It wasn't *just* their house that was boring – their clothes came from a catalogue called:

The B. Boring & Co. Catalogue
(Dressmakers to the Useless)

The B. Boring & Co. catalogues didn't use PEOPLE as models; they just showed their clothes hanging on coat hangers.

They didn't want them to look too interesting or all the useless people would stop buying them.

Now, although Aunty Prin and Aunty Min LOOKED quite similar, they couldn't have been more different. Aunty Min was by far the nicest of the two – in a boring sort of way. She was quiet and rather sweet and had a tiny squeaky voice that sounded as if it was hiding somewhere inside her body and was too afraid to come out.

Aunty Prin, on the other hand, was one of those people who seemed to enjoy being bad tempered. Her voice was spiky and crotchety and not at all afraid to come out. In fact, it was *so* crotchety it needed a special word to describe it, and the word was this: SNICKERTY.

Aggie visited Aunty Prin and Aunty Min once a fortnight and always on a Sunday at 2 o'clock. The visits were always the same: Aggie would arrive, neat and smart in her Sunday best, and sit down in the armchair in the front room.

The two aunties would be sitting where they always sat, side-by-side on the raggedy sofa watching the TV.

The programmes they watched were usually about cheese or iron filings. The reason they liked programmes about iron filings was because iron filings were so DULL, and to boring people, DULL is beautiful. The reason they liked the cheese programmes was anybody's guess.

At 3 o'clock Aunty Prin would interrupt her chain of snickerting to announce that it was:

Tea-time

and go into the kitchen and bring out an old grey plate on which were laid three sardines. She would then place the plate on the table in front of them.

10

Then it was Aunty Min's turn to speak.

Help yourself to a sardine,

she would squeak. At which point Aggie would say:

Thank you,

help herself to a slithery old sardine and eat it as quickly as she could.

Tea over, the aunties would then wipe their hands on a piece of B. Boring & Co. grey kitchen paper and continue watching the television.

At 4 o'clock the doorbell would ring and it would be Aggie's mum who had come to take her home.

Aggie would then say, "Goodbye. Oh . . . and thanks for the sardine."

All in all, Aggie had visited her aunties 78 times and every time the visit had been exactly the same. (Except on one Sunday when they had forgotten to buy sardines and Aggie had to have a pilchard instead.)

You may at this point be thinking to yourselves, "A sardine! how perfectly dreadful. Why didn't Aggie say something? Why didn't she tell those silly aunties how blummin' useless they were?"

Well you see, Aggie, was very polite. She knew that telling them something like that might hurt their feelings and useless as they were, she could never do a thing like that.

One Monday afternoon Aggie was feeling particularly sad. In fact her mouth was turning down so much at the corners that it had started to go off the edge of her face. And this was why: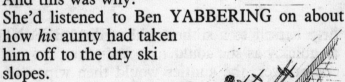
She'd listened to Ben YABBERING on about how *his* aunty had taken him off to the dry ski slopes.

She'd listened to Amy **JABBERING** on about how *her* aunty had taken her up in a hot air balloon.

And she'd listened to Nerada **BLABBERING** on about how *his* aunty had taken him to a pop concert.

All this YABBERING, JABBERING and BLABBERING had made Aggie decide that she'd had enough. Something had to be done about Aunty Prin, Aunty Min and their slithery old sardines! BUT WHAT?

After school, Aggie walked home past the sweet-shop just as she always did. In the window of the sweetshop was a noticeboard and on this noticeboard there were all kinds of cards and posters. It was something that Aggie had seen a million times before and had never once looked at twice.

But today something was different. Something MADE her look twice.

Her eyes peered through the grubby glass.

she said and looked a little closer.

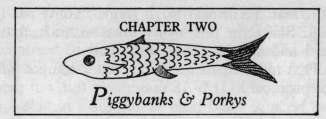

Piggybanks & Porkys

Here was the answer to all Aggie's aunty problems. She wrote the details down on the back of her hand and ran all the way home.

That night Aggie sat in her room and got out her piggybank. It WAS reasonably full, but that was because she'd been saving for a bicycle for six months. She thought about all the sweets she hadn't eaten and all the toys she hadn't bought. And then she thought about two new, improved, thoroughly re-conditioned aunties!

It would be just like taking an old pair of trousers to the dry cleaners. Brilliant!

Except that . . . an old pair of trousers couldn't say:

Go away!
We're not going to
the dry cleaners

OR

How dare you
tell a pair of trousers
what to do . . .

And you wouldn't be hurting the old pair of trousers' feelings by telling them that they were useless . . .

Don't be
too sure
about that
sunshine!

Aggie's smile faded. There was nothing else for it, she was going to have to tell her aunties that they were useless. How else would she explain the fact that she was taking them to an Academy of Advanced Auntiness?

She could almost see their hurt little faces.

It was impossible; there was no way that Aggie could do such a thing.

UNLESS . . . she didn't actually tell them that she was taking them to an Academy of Advanced Auntiness. UNLESS she told them a great big juicy fat . . .

PORKY.

A PORKY, as some of you may know, is a rather cheery expression for something that's not really very cheery at all. Porky is short for porky pie which is in fact – a lie. Now Aggie, like all good children, didn't like telling porkys, especially great big juicy fat ones, but she figured that under the circumstances it was the only thing she could do.

So, that night she put on her thinking cap. In no time at all she managed to think of a CORKER of a PORKY. And the CORKER of a PORKY was this: she would tell the useless aunties that she was taking them to an iron filings exhibition.

Now, this wasn't as stupid as it sounds, because, as you know, the aunties' most favourite television programmes were about iron filings, so the prospect of seeing some REAL LIVE ones would be an opportunity they wouldn't want to miss.

SO . . . on Wednesday, after school Aggie went round to the aunties' house to tell them the PORKY.

She walked up the steps to the front door and rang their B. Boring & Co. doorbell.

B. Boring & Co. doorbells didn't actually have a ring. That might have sounded too interesting for their customers! Instead they just had a very tuneless,  man's voice that said the words, "Ding Dong".

Aggie waited, her heart pounding in her ears. The door creaked open and Aunty Min's little face appeared round it.

At the sight of Aggie, the face seemed to jump ever so slightly. (*To get this effect just keep your eye on the illustration and then jolt the book up quickly.*)

"Hello Aunty Min," said Aggie with a beaming smile, "it's me Aggie. I, um, wondered if I could, um, come in and talk to you . . . just for a minute."

19

"It's not Sunday already is it?" squeaked Aunty Min.

"Oh no," began Aggie.

"Only we've not got any sardines."

"Who is it Min?" Came Aunty Prin's snitchy voice from inside the house. "Whoever it is, tell them to go away."

"But it's the niece, Prin; she says she's come to see us."

"The niece!" came Aunty Prin's voice once more. "What's she want to see us for? It's not Sunday is it?"

"No Aunty Prin!" called Aggie. "I've come today because I want to talk to you."

"Talk to us! Why would anyone want to talk to US?"

Aunty Prin's twitchy face appeared suddenly beside Aunty Min's.

We've not got any sardines.

"I know." said Aggie.
The two faces stared.
Aggie took a deep breath.
PORKY time had come.
"I came here today to . . .
to ask you if you would like
to see an iron filings exhibition
this Saturday morning."
Aunty Min's eyes widened excitedly.
"You mean see some REAL iron
filings, not just on the TV?"

20

"Yes." said Aggie.

"But that would mean we'd have to leave the house," snapped Aunty Prin, "go out in the cold, get on a horrible dirty bus, joggle around with a lot of noisy people . . ."

"Yes, but Prin," said Aunty Min, "we'd see some REAL iron filings."

It was clear from Aunty Min's expression that this would indeed be a dream come true.

Aunty Prin thought for a few moments, her mouth twitching from side to side.

Aggie and Aunty Min watched nervously.

Eventually she spoke.

"Well, I suppose it'd be a bit more interesting than cleaning the door knob."

Aunty Min smiled. "Does that mean we're going?"

"Yes, I suppose so," said Auntie Prin, "but don't expect me to enjoy myself."

"Well," said Aggie, breathing a very deep and incredibly secret sigh of relief. "That's great. I'll come and pick you up on Saturday morning; at 9 o'clock."

"Fine," said Aunty Min.

"Well, goodbye then," said Aggie happily.

"Goodbye," snapped Aunty Prin and slammed shut the Sludge Grey door (B. Boring & Co. Colour Chart).

Aggie skipped off down the path feeling very pleased with herself. Quite what she was going to do when it became glaringly obvious that they were *not* at an iron filings exhibition was anybody's guess; but for now she was just going to cross her fingers and hope that they'd be too stupid to notice, which was a distinct possibility.

Believe it or not, Aunty Prin was very excited about the outing, so excited in fact, that she circled the date on their calendar and snickerted on about nothing else until Aggie came to pick them up on Saturday morning.

Bet we don't see any iron filings. It'll probably ...

be cold and dark and all the iron filings will be ...

in nasty big ugly cabinets that we won't be able to see into ...

They caught the 24B bus and got off at the corner of Ponsby Place. Ponsby Place was a big square of posh houses that all looked the same. All, that is, except one. As soon as Aggie saw it she knew that it must be number 27.

There was no doubt about it, this had to be Aunt Augusta's Academy of Advanced Auntiness. Aggie smiled.

"Now," said Aggie quickly, "you two wait here and I'll find out what we have to do."

Aggie bound up the steps as fast as she could and rang the bell.

The speaker on the side of the door suddenly spluttered into action.

said a cheery voice.

"Hello," whispered Aggie, trying not to let the aunties hear her. "I've brought my aunties along for your course."

"Splendid!" said the voice. "Push the door when you hear the rude noise."

"What rude noise?"

There was suddenly a loud rasping raspberry of a noise and Aggie quickly pushed the door open.

The aunties looked up.

Aggie smiled nervously down.

"Well, come on then, let's go in."

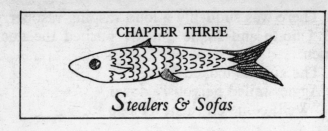

CHAPTER THREE

Stealers & Sofas

Now, if there had ever been a competition for the room that looked least like an iron filings exhibition, the reception area of Aunt Augusta's Academy of Advanced Auntiness would have won first prize. What it DID look like, was exactly what it was – a very big version of an aunty's sitting room (a REAL aunty, NOT a useless aunty. A very big version of a USELESS aunty's sitting room would look more like a rather run-down train-station waiting room that's had all its interesting furniture stolen.)

This room was most definitely the stuff of REAL aunties. Every piece of furniture had a pattern on it; every wall was festooned with all manner of hanging things and every square foot of flat surface, was home to at least twenty knick-knacks!

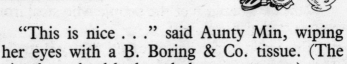

"This is nice . . ." said Aunty Min, wiping her eyes with a B. Boring & Co. tissue. (The visual overload had made her eyes water.)

"No it's not." snapped Aunty Prin, "It's frilly

and cissy and all the carpets need a good clean. And anyway, where are the iron filings?"

Aggie's smile melted away.

"Ah," she began, thinking as fast and as hard as she possibly could. "Um . . . I expect they've put them somewhere where no one can see them."

"Why would they want to do that?" asked Aunty Min, quite understandably.

"Um . . . because of the people who steal iron filings," said Aggie.

"Steal iron filings?" exclaimed Aunty Prin disbelievingly. "Who would want to steal iron filings?"

"Um . . . iron filings stealers?"

Now, this is the problem with Porkys. You can rarely get away with just telling one . . . especially one as big and fat and juicy as Aggie's.

Aggie decided that this conversation must not be continued. There was only one thing to do.

She smiled politely, took the two aunties by the hands and sat them down on the nearest sofa.

"I think it would be a good idea if you had a lovely rest while I try and convince them that you're not *stealers*.

"I know that and you know that," whispered Aggie, "but THEY don't."

Aggie then scuttled off nervously towards the reception desk. She could just make out a person behind the pile of ornaments, on the desk. Either that, or a very large lifelike knick-knack.

said the person, putting paid to the lifelike knick-knack theory.

"Hello," said Aggie, trying to keep her voice as low as possible so the aunties wouldn't hear her. "My name's Aggie and I've, um . . . brought my aunties along for your . . . um, course."

"Two, eh?" smiled Aunty Joan, attaching a very important looking form to a clipboard. "Taking advantage of our, 'Bring two, get one free' package eh? And what are their names?"

"Um . . . Aunty Prin and Aunty Min."

"And how useless would you say they were?"

"Um . . . it's . . . er, hard to say."

"Very well, I'll make it easier. If you were to give them marks out of ten, what would they get?"

Aggie thought very hard.

"Um . . . 2½."

"Is that each or both together?"

"Er . . . both together."

"BOTH TOGETHER! Oh, my dear, you haven't come a moment too soon! Now, we have a few Advanced Auntiness courses that you can choose from. There's the: '**Fat, colourful, loud, takes lots of trips and is always embarrassing course.**' The '**Slightly on the plump side, bakes lots of cakes and knits sweaters that are always the wrong size course.**' Or there's the '**Skinny, wears weird things and is almost certainly mad, course**'. Or there is our '**Bits 'n' Bobs course**'."

"What's that?"

"Well, with that one you get a bit of everything and Aunt Augusta is assisted by two people called Bob."

"Um . . . I'll take that."

"Splendid!" smiled Aunty Joan. "Two Bits 'n' Bobs."

While Aunty Joan wrote this all down, Aggie glanced nervously across at the aunties who seemed to be sinking further and further back into the big flowery sofa.

It was then that she became aware of movement around the room. A bustling jerky sort of movement that appeared to be coming from the furniture itself. Only when Aggie looked again, did she realize that this movement came from the Small, plump, jolly ladies in flowery house-

30

coats who were polishing away at anything that wasn't moving, including Aunty Prin and Aunty Min.

The reason Aggie hadn't noticed them before was that the patterns on their housecoats were SO similar to those of most of the furniture that it was actually quite difficult to see them.

To give you an idea of what I mean, see if you can find three cleaning ladies in this picture.

"I see you've noticed our marvellous worker aunts," said Aunty Joan, glancing up from her paperwork.

"Oh, yes," said Aggie.

"They never stop you know, always on the go . . . and Aunt Augusta does love to see her Academy looking spick spock span. Now, I'm afraid we've come to the rather unpleasant, part," Aunty Joan smiled apologetically.

"We have?" Aggie wondered what on earth she was about to say.

"Piggybank time."

"Oh, yes, of course. I'm sorry. Here we are."

31

Aggie quickly removed her piggybank from her bag and put it on the desk.

Aunty Joan picked it up and, with a professional air, felt the weight of it.

It's terrible that we have to charge, but I'm sure you'll be very happy with the results. Of course, there IS the piggybank money back guarantee if you're not satisfied.

"There is?" said Aggie.

"Oh yes, but we've never had to use it. I don't think we've ever had anyone who wasn't satisfied. My, my, you have been saving up, haven't you?"

Aggie nodded dolefully.

"Right then." Aunty Joan put the piggybank away, flicked a switch on the switchboard and spoke into a little microphone.

"Two to be weighed and measured Aunty Ethel."

"Righty-ho Aunty Joan!" came a voice and, the couch the aunties were sitting on span round into the wall and an auntiless couch appeared in its place.

32

EEK!

Aggie gave a little gasp.

"Now then, my dear, don't you worry a jot about those dreadful old aunties of yours, they've just gone off for a bit of weighing and measuring. They'll be back again soon."

"Oh," said Aggie, trying very hard not to think about what Aunty Prin would say to anyone who tried to weigh or measure her.

"Now, here's your sticky-on-name-tag, pop yourself over there with the others and I'll call you when your aunties are ready."

OTHERS?

"Yes others," said Aunty Joan.

Now, that was something that Aggie had never even thought about.

"You're not the only person in the world with useless aunties you know."

And indeed Aggie wasn't.

The first person Aggie saw as she approached the cosy little waiting area was a very nervous looking boy who was pacing up and down.

Aggie, politely introduced herself.

"Hello," she said, "I'm Aggie."

The boy immediately stopped pacing, grabbed Aggie's hand and shook it.

Aggie had heard voices like Bertie's before. They usually belonged to the kids who went to the posh school across the road.

"Do you think she'll be all right?" he enquired earnestly.

"Um . . . who?" asked Aggie, removing her hand from his lettuce-like grip.

"Auntie Gertiepoo. Only she's not really very used to this sort of thing, you know, having to do things for herself. She's very rich you see, and usually pays people to do things for her, like cook and clean and walk down the street."

"Walk down the street?"

"Oh yes, Auntie Gertiepoo would never walk down the street. She's got this little lady called Mrs Shrub who does it for her. She just hops in a taxi and meets her at the other end, that way she feels that she's done a bit of exercise."

"How strange," thought Aggie.

"Which was all very well and good until she started paying Mrs Shrub to do auntyish things with me so SHE wouldn't have to. Well, eventually I got a bit peevy-pooed."

Peevy-pooed?

"Oh, yes,
and I told her that
it wasn't good enough. SHE was my auntypoo and she must behave as such! And much to my surprise she agreed to come here."

Suddenly someone else spoke.

"I don't think people should be allowed to be rich," said the voice.

35

Aggie looked round. Curled up on a nearby chair was a lanky girl with big round glasses and a lot of very large teeth.

I think rich people should give all their money to poor people and old donkeys ...

"And anyway, Mr Show-off Trousers," the girl continued, "you don't have to be rich to be useless. My Aunty Lottie hasn't got two five pences to rub together and she's the most useless person I've ever met! I told her two months ago that I was bringing her here and she's done no swotting up whatsoever. I mean, I'm not handing over my hard saved piggybank money just so that lazy old dunce can sit back and do nothing."

"Sorry babe; could you say that again."

Now, THIS was a very high voice, not only in tone but also in direction.

The three children looked up.

Standing on top of a sturdy cabinet was a small wiry boy, holding a video camera.

36

Aggie had heard children say things like "babe" and "guys" and "wicked" before, but never with such a high squeaky voice. If she hadn't been so polite, she might have laughed.

"Well, I assure you we're not wicked," spluttered Bertie. "At least, I'm not. And anyway, two of us are girls."

"He means we look good," sighed Dottie. "It's some pathetic way of talking he's picked up from watching too much television."

"There is no such thing as too much television," said the boy, jumping down.

"...ly are you filming us?" asked Aggie. She could see from his sticky-on-name-tag that his name was Joe.

"I film everything," said Joe with a grin. "One day I'm going to have my own TV show and I'm going to put all this stuff in it!"

"Sounds *really* boring," sniped Dottie. "I wouldn't watch it."

"I would," said Aggie smiling and wondering why Dottie was so horrible to everyone.

"I would if it was educational," said Bertie polishing his cub scout badge.

"Hey," began Joe. "I was listening to you guys rapping on about swotting. Well, my Aunty Flo has done some Mega-swotting. It's like, Homework City back at her place."

"Homework City?" said Bertie. "Where's that then?"

"He means, moneybrains, that his aunty has done a lot of work," said Dottie, looking suddenly rather uncomfortable.

"Not that my aunty hasn't. When I said she *hadn't* swotted, what I meant was . . ."

At that moment a voice rang out behind them.

Children, your aunties are ready.

The children looked round, and sure enough, there they were, all standing in a line and all wearing what looked like big flowery dresses over their clothes.

All except one, who appeared to be wearing a pair of spotted bloomers and a balaclava helmet. Aggie knew immediately from the large round glasses whose aunty she was.

"Why is that one dressed differently from the others?" muttered Bertie.

"Because . . ." began Dottie, in her now familiar know-it-all voice. "She's doing the 'Skinny, wears wierd things and is almost certainly mad course'. I thought the 'Bits 'n' Bobs' sounded a bit cheapo!"

"CHEAPO!" exploded Bertie. "I can't have Aunty Gertie doing something CHEAPO! She'll never forgive me!"

"Chill out man," squeaked Joe. "The Bits 'n' Bobs is Cool City. That's what my aunty's doing."

"And mine," added Aggie, hardly daring to

look at Aunty Prin and Aunty Min. When she did she got quite a surprise. "They look as if they've put on about fifteen stone," she gasped.

"Padded auntysuits," said Aunty Joan. "Makes the skinny ones look a bit more jolly. Now, then, why don't you all go and have a lovely chit, chat, choo to your aunties before Aunt Augusta arrives."

Aggie's heart fell. A lovely "chit, chat, choo" was the last thing she was going to have, judging by the expression on Aunty Prin's face, but she walked across.

"Everything all right?" she said, forcing a smile.

Yes, lovely. These padded things are very nice.

No they're not. They're horrid and squishy and they make us look like big fat elephants, and anyway why are we wearing them?

"Um . . ." Aggie didn't have the first idea what she was going to say, she just opened her mouth and waited to see what came out.

"So why have we just been weighed and measured then?" snapped Aunty Prin.

"Um . . . I think it's quite a small exhibition and they need to know if you'll fit in the room."

"Did you tell them that we weren't stealers?" asked little Aunty Min.

"Oh yes, I told them."

The PORKYS were coming thick and fast. It was no good, Aggie knew that she was going to have to tell them the truth soon. She was just about to decide when, where and how, when she suddenly became aware of a distant clacking noise like high heeled footsteps.

Dottie stood in front of her Aunty Lottie and jabbed her with a finger.

41

"Because," hissed Dottie through her tombstone teeth, "you're doing the 'Skinny and mad course'. I got you the easy one, remember. I mean, you're already skinny and you're at least half mad."

The sound of high heeled footsteps was now joined by a faint jingling sound.

Bertie's aunty looked down at her trembling nephew.

"Bertiepoo!" she trilled, "that woman over there has got a notebook and pencils. AND she's got a nice shiny satchel. Why haven't I got a nice shiny satchel? Look here's a thousand pounds; go and get me one of those satchels and make sure it's bigger and shinier than hers."

"But I can't go out now," wailed Bertie. "Aunt Augusta's on her way."

I don't care if the Queenypoo's on her way, I want one of those shiny satchels, and I want one NOW!

43

The footsteps and jingling were now joined by the sound of swooshing petticoats.

Joe was filming his Aunty Flo with his video camera.

"So Aunty Flo," he said, "how are you feeling?"

"I feel very confident Joe. I've done my home-work, I feel ready to face the course. Test me, go on, ask me a question."

"Um," Joe zoomed in on her face. "O.K. What is a knick-knack?"

Auntie Flo thought for a few seconds.

A small decorative, completely useless object.

"Good!" beamed Joe, taking the camera down from his face. "Aunty City here we come!"

The footsteps and the jingling and the swooshing were about as close as they could be without actually being in the room.

Suddenly, there was a very sweet smell. Aunty Joan breathed it in and smiled. The worker aunts quickly stood in a line.

The door handle rattled. The door opened and there, in a cloud of powder and perfume stood the flounciest, floweryest, softest, sweetest, cosiest, cheerfulest, jinglyest, janglyest . . . AUNTIEST person anyone had ever seen in the whole of their lives.

This was, of course, Aunt Augusta.

The worker aunts and Aunty Joan gazed proudly at their mistress.

Now, if you'd gone along the line of useless aunties at that moment and asked them all to write down their first impressions of Aunt Augusta, this is what they would have put:

NAME	FIRST IMPRESSION
Auntie Flo	Looks as if she knows what she's doing . . .
Auntie Gertie	Her jewellery's made of plastic – doesn't look very highly qualified to me . . .
Auntie Lottie	I hope she doesn't shout at me . . .
Auntie Min	Very nice . . .
Auntie Prin	She looks like a fat over-stuffed armchair and anyway who the blummin' heck is she?

Aunt Augusta's voice trilled round the room.

"Hellooo, my most jellyest of babies, my most jammyest of dodgers, my most knickerbockerest of glories, helloooo and welcome to . . . Auntyland."

She then gave everyone a smile as wide as a very large boomerang.

"So, what have we got today then Aunty Joan?" she said, casting a beaming smile along the little row of aunties.

"Four 'Bits 'n' Bobs' and one 'Skinny and mad', Aunt Augusta," said Aunty Joan.

"All got sticky-on-name-tags?"

Aunty Joan nodded.

"Marvellous!" said Aunt Augusta, beaming and clapping her surprisingly small hands together with glee. "The Bobs will be soooo pleased!"

Aggie had been so entranced by Aunt Augusta's entrance that she'd almost forgotten about all the horrible PORKY stuff, but something suddenly reminded her!

Excuse me.

"Oh no," thought Aggie, "what could she possibly be about to say?"

"Yes?" smiled Aunt Augusta.

47

"I'm sure I speak for all of us," began Aunty Prin, "when I say that we've been here for over an hour now and we've not seen one iron filing."

Everyone looked slowly and quizzically round at Aunty Prin.

Aggie's mouth went completely dry.

After a few seconds Aunt Augusta's face suddenly split into a wide smile, "what a marvellous skinny and mad thing to say!"

"I *beg* your pardon?" squawked Aunty Prin.

". . . and we're not even in the classroom yet. How splendidly splendid! Two stars for the Skinny and Mad!"

"Um, I don't think she's actually doing the skin . . ." began Aunty Joan running a finger down her clipboard. But it was too late, Aunt Augusta was off, one arm round Aunty Prin's shoulder and the other waving high in the air.

"Come on everyone, follow me."

48

Aggie kept as near to the back as she could. She had a feeling that as soon as Aunty Prin escaped Aunt Augusta's clutches she would be heading for Explanation City as Joe would say.

After a few moments, Aunt Augusta stopped in front of a large wooden door.

"Now my wonderful aunties-to-be," she beamed, "we have arrived at the first port of call on the road to 'complete and utter auntiness'. You see, in order to go forwards we must first go back; into the mists of time. In other words we must take a peeky-boo at our AUNTCESTORS."

An excited hush had fallen on the little group.

"So follow me," she whispered, "into . . . THE AUNT GALLERY."

"Mmmm very nice," squeaked Aunty Min and the door began to open.

CHAPTER FIVE

Curiosities & Confessions

The Aunt Gallery was very much like a museum except that it was full of Auntyish things. Once inside, Aunt Augusta addressed the little group again.

She was probably saying some very interesting things but inside Aggie's head all she could hear was:

The PORKY was beginning to get to her, which is something that often happens with PORKYS.

It didn't help that Aunty Prin was now standing a few yards away, snickerting into Aunty Min's ear.

"Oh, no." thought Aggie. This had really gone far enough. There was nothing else for it, the truth was going to have to be told.

SO; while everyone was busy listening to Aunt Augusta, Aggie did something that really wasn't very polite. She grabbed her two aunties by the hands and quickly pulled them behind a very large glass cabinet.

"What the . . ." began Aunty Prin.

Aggie quickly put her finger to her mouth.

"Shhhh, I'm sorry, I really am, but there's something I've GOT to tell you."

"What?" snapped Aunty Prin.
"What is it?" squeaked Aunty Min.
Both the aunties looked at Aggie.
Aggie took a deep breath.

This isn't an iron filings exhibition.

"Isn't it?" exclaimed Aunty Min in extreme disbelief.

"No." Aggie shook her head.

"Well, what *is* it then?" said Aunty Prin.

Aggie could hear the crowd moving away into another room.

"It's . . . Aunt Augusta's Academy for Advanced Auntiness. It's a place where people go to learn how to be proper aunties."

There was a short pause and then Aunty Prin spoke.

"So why did you bring US here then?"

Aggie looked at the two aunties. They genuinely had no idea.

"Because . . ."

Aggie would have preferred to do anything in the world rather than answer that question.

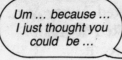

Um ... because ...
I just thought you
could be ...

Um . . . I MEAN
it's not that
you're not er ...

It's just that
with a bit of teaching,
you know ... a few tips
you could REALLY be ...
um you know sort of ...

Aunty Prin's eyes suddenly narrowed.

"Are you trying to say that your Aunty Min and I aren't very good aunties?"

"Oh, no," said Aggie. "No, you're fine. Well, when I say fine, I mean . . . you're O.K., just a bit sort of um . . . er . . . well um . . . a bit, er . . . well, actually I suppose yes, that is what I'm saying . . ."

54

"WHAT!" exploded Aunty Prin. Aggie looked down at the ground.

"Oh, dear," said Aunty Min, obviously quite upset. "Well, what are we doing wrong?"

"Oh nothing," said Aggie. "Well, when I say nothing, I mean, maybe just a few things, you know, little things, tiny weeny things like, um, you know . . . you don't take me out on trips."

"We thought you liked sardines," squeaked Aunty Min.

"Um . . . I do, I love sardines . . . but . . . it's not really enough."

"You could have had *two* sardines."

"No," laughed Aggie hopelessly, "you don't understand." She looked up into their faces. Even crotchety old Aunty Prin was beginning to look a bit sad.

It was no good this was going to be impossible.

"Look," said Aggie, "it really doesn't matter, I was wrong to bring you here; you don't have to do this; you're fine you REALLY are; let's just forget it and go home, come on let's go home now."

Aggie turned and began to walk back towards the door. She had a horrible feeling that she was about to cry.

"You're right," came Aunty Prin's voice suddenly from behind her.

"I beg your pardon?"

Aggie turned back.

Aunty Prin was looking down at the ground.

"I said, you're right, we're not very good aunties, in fact we're blummin' terrible."

"Are we?" squeaked Aunty Min.

"Of course we are you silly old turnip. We can't help it, it's just the way we've been made I suppose. Look niece, if it will make you happy we'll try and do this aunty course of yours.

Now we come to more recent history. I think the emergence of aunties as we know them can best be illustrated

You're the only one who comes and visits us and if you stopped coming . . . we'd possibly never see anyone again."

Aggie looked from one aunty to the other and smiled.

"You mean you'll *really* do it?" she said.

"I said we'd TRY." And with that, Aunty Prin gave the nearest thing to a smile Aggie had ever seen. Aggie gave them both a little hug.

"Thanks," she said.

"Does that mean we won't be seeing any iron filings?" squeaked Aunty Min.

★

The rest of the party had moved through to the main part of the museum. Aunt Augusta was still in full flow. Aggie and the two aunties crept in and stood behind them.

by a hop skip and a jump through the life and times of one of the best known and best-loved aunties who has ever lived:

my namesake aunty – Aunt Augusta the First! Now why do you think she was everyone's favourite Aunty?

Because she always had a little something in her bag for all little children?

"Absolutely correct Aunty Flo. That woman could be surrounded by sixty children and she'd still have a little something in her bag for each and every one of them."

"She must have had a big bag," muttered Bertie.

"She certainly did," said Aunt Augusta, smiling, "and there it is."

"Now follow me and we shall see a few of the other things that made her so marvellously marvellous."

It was then that Aggie, and just about everyone else, realized that Aunt Augusta was one of those people who liked to do things very fast.

Here are some of her marvellous hats.

Here is some of her marvellous jewellery.

Here are some of her marvellous dresses.

Here are some of her marvellous knick knacks.

And here are some of her marvellous woolleys.

In one and a half minutes they saw more marvellous objects than they had ever seen in their lives before. Suddenly, Aunt Augusta screeched to a halt and pointed upwards.

"And there she is, the marvellous woman her-self, Aunt Augusta the First."
Everyone looked and everyone gasped.

She was indeed an extraordinary sight.

"Is that what the niece wants US to look like?" squeaked Aunty Min.

"I blummin' well hope not," snapped Aunty Prin, "she looks like she's swallowed a duvet!"

"What's that hanging from her nose?" said Aunty Gertie. "It looks like some horrible big bogeypoo."

Aunt Augusta's face suddenly became sad.

"If only . . ." she said, and then slowly lowered herself on to a chair. From the tone of her voice, everyone knew that a story was about to be told.

"Now, as I'm sure you all know," she began, "every aunty worth her salt must have a party piece."

Of course.

"And Aunt Augusta's was, of course, the finest of them all. Well, one day she was doing it at one of her nephew's birthday parties. There she was, in full flow kicking those marvellous old legs of hers high up into the air, when, suddenly, a terrible thing happened; her right leg flew up much higher than usual and the pointy toe of her shoe went straight up her nose.

"Being the *real* Aunty she was, she carried on singing and dancing, trying every now and then to pull the shoe out. She even made up a song, on the spot, called *I've got a shoe dangling out of my nose!* so the little children wouldn't be alarmed. But try as she might, she could not pull that shoe from her poor, poor nostril. A doctor was called; the fire brigade was called; but it was no good, nobody could get it out. The awful thing was that she couldn't be an aunty any more. You can't have an aunty with a size five winklepicker dangling from her nosey. It's just not done, so she retired to an old aunties' home, never to be seen again."

With that Aunt Augusta collapsed sobbing into her hankie.

"Wow, heavy," said Joe.

"I expect it was." said Bertie. "Mind you, it could have been worse, it could have been a wellington."

Suddenly, Aunt Augusta's head re-appeared.

"RIGHT!" she said, recovering quite dramatically from her sorrow. "It is now time to leave the past and return to the present." She sprang to her feet, pushed open the nearest door and marched out into the corridor.

The time has come for us to embark on the first part of our Advanced Auntiness Course! Please remember this is a very condensed course, which means we have a lot to do in a very short time ... so we must all pay attention or we won't get our diplomas will we?

"Diplomas!" yelped Dottie. "I didn't know there were diplomas," she turned and snarled at Aunty Lottie.

"Couldn't you have read just one book!"

"Oh yes!" said Aunt Augusta, beaming, there's lots of lovely diplomas, four grades in all, *plus* the Golden Knick-Knack for showing the most promise."

"So, everyone spick, spock, span, and ready to go?" asked Aunt Augusta with a smile.

Nine heads nodded.

"So follow me to the place where auntiness begins."

CHAPTER SIX

Softus, Sweetus, Sloppyus

"The place where auntiness begins" looked very much like a classroom, except for one thing. It was painted bright pink.

"Is this where we're supposed to sit?" shrieked Aunty Gertie. "At these deskipoos! They're all

65

wooden, and these chairs are so hard. Isn't there a padded armchair I could use, I'll pay extra."

"My dear lady," smiled Aunt Augusta. "We are here to LEARN not LOUNGE ABOUT! Now everyone into your seats!"

"Do you think there's a special Skinny and Mad desk?" muttered Aunty Lottie, hoping REALLY hard that there wasn't.

Aunty Flo sat down and immediately started setting out her desk. When she'd finished, it looked like this:

Neat eh?

"It's like being back at school isn't it, Prin." chuckled little Aunty Min settling down into her seat.

"No it's not," snapped Aunty Prin. "It's nothing like being back at school. Little Jimmy Scrogget isn't here for one thing. AND it doesn't smell of old toenails."

Aggie glanced across at the aunties and was quite relieved to see that Aunty Prin was snickerting away happily.

"Everything's going to be all right," she thought.

Just then she became aware of a rumbling noise, like giant's footsteps, then all at once . . .

the floorboards began to shake . . .

the desks began to rattle and . . .

the lights began to flicker.

Suddenly, from the back of the class, two huge shapes began to emerge.

BOBS WARNING! BOBS WARNING!
BOBS WARNING! BOBS WARNING!

These huge shapes were in fact, the BOBS.

Now, before we go any further, allow me to tell you a bit about the Bobs. The Bobs were Aunt Augusta's favourite nephews, and they were very fat; very, very fat. In fact, I would go so far as to say that in the history of English literature there have never been two boys as fat as the Bobs. They made Tweedledum and Tweedledee look like matchstick men.

Actually "fat" is probably *too* neat a word to describe the Bobs. A more accurate description might be: "squidgidy squadgidy" or "wibbledy  wobbledy" or perhaps best of all, "flibbily, flobbily, flabbily" . . . "flollop!"

In fact the Bobs are SO flibbily, flobbily, flabbily, flollop, it is very difficult to fit them into our illustrations but I'll do the best I can.

The Bobs at the seaside.   *The Bobs collecting stamps.*   *The Bobs at Christmas.*

Aunt Augusta spotted the Bobs at once. (It was actually quite difficult not to.)

"Well look who's here to greet us!" she boomed.

"Wobble City," muttered Joe, changing his lens to wide-angle.

"Look at our teeth Aunty," gushed the Bobs, "and see how round our tummies are."

Oh yes! They are coming on a treat! See these, ladies, THEY are tummies full of love,

and see these lovely brown teeth, kisses from the love fairy, that's what they are.

They both tell the world that you've got an aunty who loves you ...

"How very odd." thought Aggie. She'd always been taught that it wasn't very healthy to be fat and have bad teeth. But perhaps Aunt Augusta knew something that she didn't.

Aunt Augusta shooed the Bobs back to where they came from and faced her class.

"Now Aunties, we MUST get on. First of all, let us ask ourselves this question: What is an aunty? . . . Aunty Min?"

Um . . . she's a big fat lady who wears horrible clothes and gives children lots of sweets.

'She most certainly is not!" snapped Aunt Augusta, aghast. "Big fat lady indeed! Aunty Flo?"

"Someone who's soft to cuddle, always gives you something sweet and can sometimes go all sloppy," recited Aunty Flo.

"Absolutely right. So from now on, these MUST be your bywords: Soft, sweet and sloppy. You see how important they are. Look up there, on our coat of arms; there they are in Latin; Softus, Sweetus et Sloppyus."

"Excuse me," came Bertie's voice. "That's not Latin, you've just put a *us* on the end of every word."

Aunt Augusta's face suddenly looked a bit sour.

"Well spotted my dear and so highly intelligent child. When I say *Latin*, what I MEAN is, Auntylatin, a very different language altogether, rather like Auntyspeak. And talking of Auntyspeak I want you all to open your desks. Inside you will find an Auntyspeak Dictionary."

"Is it all right if I use my own copy?" asked Aunty Flo, pulling a well thumbed copy from her satchel.

"Of course my dear," said Aunt Augusta, clearly impressed.

It was then that Aunty Gertie, who was getting very irritated by Aunty Flo's cleverness, did a very childish thing. She impersonated Aunty Flo's voice.

Luckily Aunt Augusta didn't notice.

"Inside the dictionary you will find all kinds of special aunty words like, jingly-janglies, swishy-swooshies and choochie-woochies; so let's keep it handy.

"Now, we're not going to bother with the Cheek Chukker as even the most useless aunty knows how to do that."

Aunty Prin and Aunty Min looked at each other and shrugged.

(*Once again: to get this effect . . . keep your eyes on Aunty Prin and Aunty Min's shoulders only and jolt the book up quickly.*)

"So, let's get straight on to the Smackeroo. Who knows what a Smackeroo is? . . . Aunty Gertie?"

"Well, it's a jolly good smack isn't it?"

"My goodness me!" shrieked Aunt Augusta, clearly shaken. "Never let me hear you say those words again, especially in front of my Bobs. Aunty Flo?"

"It's an aunty kiss," said Aunty Flo, looking smugly round at Aunty Gertie who sank back into her chair and chewed her lip.

"Yes, of course it is Aunty Flo. Lots of gold stars for that. Now come, everyone up on their feet and let's try the smackeroo. Nieces and neffys in front of your aunties. Now where's our lovely Skinny and Mad?"

"Here she is!" squawked Dottie, pushing her nervous looking aunty forwards.

Now my dear, Skinny and Mad smackeroos are different from Bits 'n' Bobs smackeroos. Allow me to demonstrate.

Grab the niece by the shoulders ...

-MWA!-

and miss the face completely! Just kiss the air

-MWA!-

"OOF!

either side of her face.

73

"Got that?"

Aunty Lottie nodded.

"You better have done," hissed Dottie.

"Now then, everyone else . . ." trilled Aunt Augusta.

"Excuse me . . ." began Aunty Gertie. "We're not actually going to have to kiss the nephewipoo are we? It's just that I've got my favourite lipstick on."

"My dear woman, cuddling is far more important than cosmetics, and, anyway, how do you usually manage?"

"Well, I don't think Mrs Shrub wears lipstick does she Bertiepoo?"

"Please Aunty Gertie, just pay attention and do what I say. First positions, and spot the niece or neffy and . . .

eyes open wide . . .

Ninety degrees I believe is correct.

arms open wide . . .

74

nice big smile . . .

pout like a codfish and . . .
SMACKEROOOOO!"

Everyone smackerooed.
Mwaaaaaa!
There was a sound in the room like a swarm
of bees followed by a massive gasp as everyone
finished.

"Marvellous, marvellous everyone . . ." applauded Aunt Augusta, beaming.

"Right, while we're all still in the mood. Does anyone know something else we use an aunty kiss for?"

Aunty Flo put up her hand.

"To kiss things better."

"Quite right!" said Aunt Augusta. "There is nothing that can stop pain and discomfort more quickly than a lovely old smackeroo on the injured area. You can keep all your pain killers and your aspirins. A smackeroo a day keeps the doctor away."

Just then, Aggie noticed that Aunty Prin's hand was up again.

"Excuse me," came her crotchety voice, "but what if the child's broken an arm or something?"

Aunt Augusta looked round slowly.

"You couldn't kiss it better then, could you? I mean it wouldn't make any difference. It's hardly going to mend a bone is it?"

The expression on Aunt Augusta's face would have made a charging rhinoceros turn and head off in the other direction.

Ooer, I'm off.

"No," she barked. "No, it probably wouldn't."

She stared at Aunty Prin for a few seconds then she suddenly picked up a small handbell and rang it very loudly.

"Right then," she said. "Time to move on to our Aunts and Crafts section. While I get the classroom ready my marvellous Bobs will keep you entranced with some of their wonderful Jelly Juggling."

Aggie looked up slowly at Aunty Prin.

"Um . . . Why did you say that? None of the other aunties said anything like that."

"I said it niece," said Aunty Prin, "because it needed to be said."

Aunty Min gave a little nod.

Aggie's vision of her aunties accepting the Golden Knick-Knack was beginning to fade a little round the edges.

Suddenly, there were two very large wobbles followed by a series of very small wobbles as the Bobs prepared to launch a selection of gleaming yellow table jellies into the air.

CHAPTER SEVEN

Notes & Knatty Knitters

"I'm getting a little bit tired of old swotty-pants over there." muttered Aunty Gertie, flicking a manicured finger in the direction of Aunty Flo.

"Please Aunty Gertiepoo," jibbered Bertie, "don't do anything naughty; you won't get the Golden Knick-Knack . . ."

Now then, my lovely aunties-to-be . . .

Aunt Augusta clapped her hands. Behind her stood four mysterious looking objects.

"It's time for you to learn some aunty crafts. And what is the most famous aunty craft of all?"

"Woollies," said Aunty Flo.

"It most certainly is; and as we all know, auntymade things are the best made things because they don't come from shops do they Aunty Gertie?"

"Don't they?"

"Oh no, they come from the heart."

"Oh pass the sickypoo-bag."

"Aunty Gertiepoo!" yelped Bertie.

"Right then," continued Aunt Augusta, "it's our lovely niece or nephew's birthday. We are going to knit them a wonderful woolly . . . so . . . what's the first thing we are going to need?"

Aunt Augusta's face lit up. "What a marvellous Skinny and Mad answer Aunty Lottie. Of course, it's wrong but a gold star for trying."

Aunty Lottie was just about to explain that eating kippers helped her to think when Dottie whispered in her ear.

"And the REAL answer is? . . . Aunty Flo?"

"To find out what their favourite cartoon character is."

"Good, Aunty Flo." gushed Aunt Augusta. "You HAVE been doing your homework. You see, you need to know their favourite cartoon character, so you can knit the cheeky little critter's face on the front of the woolly," said Aunt Augusta, smiling.

Now, it was while Aunt Augusta was saying those words and everybody was watching her, that Aunty Gertie decided to do something very naughty indeed.

This naughty thing involved her hand and Aunty Flo's notes:

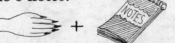 +

so, no more notes for Aunty Flo!

81

"Right then," trilled Aunt Augusta. "Let's find out what they are. One at a time please . . . Joe?"

Well, that's like, well tricky, because a cartoon character could be like, Trend City one day and then slacksville the next . . . and like, your street credibility could WELL plummet if you're like, sighted with yesterday's dude on your woolly!

"Joe," coaxed Aunt Augusta with a smile, "could you speak in English please."

"Sorry Aunt Augusta," squeaked Joe. "It's Cool Man."

"Yes I know but could you tell me your character?"

"No, that's his name, 'Cool Man', you know, like Superman."

"Very well. Everyone else?"

Billy the invisible boy and his Magic Stick.

The Man Who Reads the News.

I'll choose something easy . . .

I say, what's a cartoon character?

Bagrat the Four-headed, Pig-snouted, Five-eyed Multicoloured Mongasaurus.

I'll give that old dunce something really skinny and mad!

"Oh dearie me," sighed Aunty Lottie, trying very hard to imagine what Bagrat the four-headed, pig-snouted, five-eyed, multicoloured Mongasaurus looked like.

"Right then, so what's the next thing we need to do? . . . Aunty Flo?" asked Aunt Augusta, still smiling.

Aunty Flo looked very flustered. "Um . . . I'm sorry, I can't seem to find my notes."

"Well don't worry, just try and answer the question."

"Um . . . find out their size?"

"Oh, Aunty Flo. I'm disappointed in you. That is one thing we must never do. On NO account must you EVER find out the size of your niece or nephew. Imagine their disappointment on opening your marvellously wrapped present only to discover that it actually fitted!"

"Oh yeuch!" exclaimed Aunty Gertie, amidst a rustle of paper.

"Well you tell us then Aunty Gertie."

"You have to decide whether you want it to be too big or too small."

"Good, Aunty Gertie . . . a gold star!"

Aunty Gertie smiled smugly across at Aunty Flo who'd tipped her shiny satchel upside-down and was now scrabbling about on the floor, trying to find her notes.

"Now, if you were to REALLY knit your woollies, the whole process could take months, which we don't have. So we use these." Aunt Augusta pointed at the machines. "Aunt Augusta's Knatty Knitters."

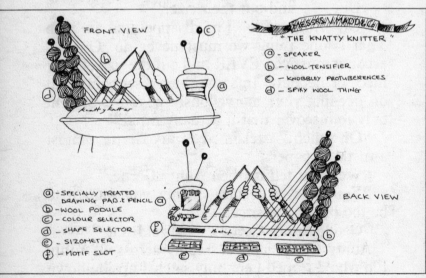

"WOW!" said Joe. "Hi-tech City!"

"With these little wonders, we can whip up a woolly in a wee while. SO Aunties, to your machines. Oh yes, Aunty Lottie, yours is the one with the plastic lobsters on it!"

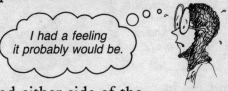

I had a feeling it probably would be.

The Bobs stood either side of the Knatty Knitters, chequered flags at the ready.
The aunties sat down.

At the side of the knatty knitters you will see a little drawing pad, on which I want you to draw a picture of your cartoon character. Then insert it in the slot marked motif!

"But how do we know what these cartoon characters look like?" wailed little Aunty Min.

"My word, you are a slacker Aunty Min. It is

an aunty's job to keep up with all the latest cartoon characters. Dear me. Now, pick up your pencils . . .

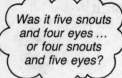

"And ready . . .

"Steady . . .

"Dogs gone to beddy . . .

"and . . .

The Bobs brought down the flags and the aunties were off!

The children cheered them on . . .

"And insert the drawing into your slots marked MOTIF!" shrieked Aunt Augusta, skipping around excitedly.

The machines slurped up the sketches and the size buttons began to flash almost immediately.

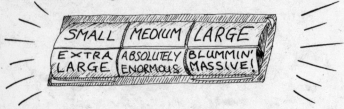

| SMALL | MEDIUM | LARGE |
| EXTRA LARGE | ABSOLUTELY ENORMOUS | BLUMMIN' MASSIVE! |

"Now punch in your shapes and colours . . ."

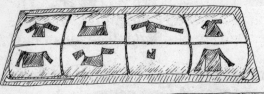

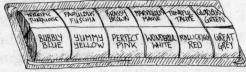

| TERRIFIC TURQUOISE | FABULOUS FUSCHIA | BRASSY BROWN | MARVELLOUS MAUVE | TUNEFUL TAUPE | GLORIOUS GREEN |
| BUBBLY BLUE | YUMMY YELLOW | PERFECT PINK | WONDERFUL WHITE | ROLLICKING RED | GREAT GREY |

"Now sit back and watch those machines GO!"

AND . . . the knitting began to appear. The aunties watched in astonishment as 50 little needles jabbed and spun through the taut strands of wool.

"Come on!" screamed the children, clambering up on to their desks for a better view.

The finished woollies fell to the ground with a triple somersault.

Aggie smiled across at her aunties; theirs was easily the best.

The Bobs skipped across and picked them all up.

"Now nieces and nephews, on with your woollies and let's see whose is the most Auntymade."

The aunties watched anxiously as the children struggled into them. Aunt Augusta ushered them to the front.

"Well, I would say there was no contest." said Aunt Augusta, smiling. "It's sweet, it's soft, it's sloppy; it's the most Auntymade of all. Bobs tell them."

Everyone held their breath.

"It's Aunty Flo's!" chorused the Bobs.

"Yes!" cheered Joe handing his camera to Bertie and asking him to film him in "Winning Woolley City".

Sorry, but which end do I look through?

90

Aunty Flo was beside herself with joy.

Aunty Prin's eyes began to narrow, her hand began to rise, her voice began to speak.

"Um . . . I'm sorry," she said, "but wouldn't the little children feel a bit embarrassed wearing such a horrible looking jumper?"

Aunt Augusta turned slowly round. The expression on her face would have made the Creature-who-slurped-out-of-the-Black-Lagoon decide to slurp back in again.

Er, actually on second thoughts . . .

Aunty Prin continued. "Well, it's such a mess isn't it?"

Aunty Flo clapped her hand over her mouth in horror.

Aunt Augusta's voice was very low and very shaky, "I will choose to ignore that very unauntyish remark. Time is moving on and we must embark on the next part of our course which will take place on the Aunty Outing Training Ground."

"Aunty Outing Training Ground?" gasped Dottie. "Does that mean we're going to go outside?"

"We most certainly are."

"This sounds like a job for Mrs Shrub, Bertiepoo!" muttered Aunty Gertie.

"Oh no it doesn't, and by the way I put those notes back in Aunty Flo's desk."

"You're a horrid little spoilsport Bertiepoo!"

"Now," said the beaming Aunt Augusta, "I will go on ahead and prepare the course. Meanwhile, nieces' and neffys' coats and hats on. As usual my marvellous Bobs will keep you entertained with their magnificent 'Dance of The Seventeen Sandwiches'. With that she strode through the door and slammed it soundly behind her.

*

Aggie looked disbelievingly up at Aunty Prin, who kept her eyes down and ran her finger across the finished woolly.

"I think this sweater looks very nice, don't you Min?"

Aunty Min nodded.

"Very nice indeed." she said.

CHAPTER EIGHT

Cardboard & Cauliflowers

This is a map of the Aunty Outing Training Ground:

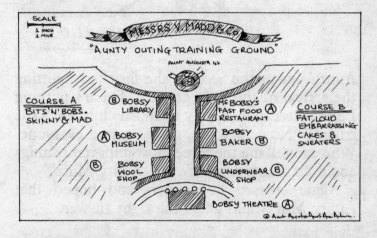

It looked at first glance like a normal street. BUT, if you looked closely you could see that it wasn't actually a normal street at all; it was completely pretend. Everything was made out of painted wood, just like something you might see on a stage.

At the entrance stood a cardboard statue of Aunt Augusta the First. In front of this stood

MARVELLOUS!

Aunt Augusta the Second: she shrieked, spotting the arrival of the little group. "There's nothing I like better than freshly wrapped children," she trilled. "Now come on, gather round everyone. Who can tell me the three most important things about an Aunty Outing? . . . Aunty Min?"

Aggie crossed her fingers and hoped that Aunty Min would guess the right answer.

Um ... never step in puddles, keep your back to the butchers and always take a spare bag of grated cheese.

"What complete and utter nonsense. You REALLY have no idea do you?"

"Well, I'm sure Aunty Flo can tell us."

"Well, yes, I can now that Aunty Gertie has returned my notes."

"What?"

"How did you? I mean, you little tell tale."

"Well, at least I'm not a cheat!"

Then Aunty Flo pulled this face at Aunty Gertie . . .

and Aunty Gertie pulled this face at Aunty Flo. The children watched in amazement.

"Ladies please!" shrieked Aunt Augusta. "Enough of this, we must get on. Now where was I? Oh yes, the three most important things about Aunty Outings are . . ."

"To go to as many places as you can, eat as much as you can, as quickly as you can." Aunty Flo grinned and pulled another very quick face at Aunty Gertie.

"Very good."

"Excuse me," said Aunty Lottie. "Do Skinny and Mad aunties do normal outings? It's just that I had this idea to make the outing more Skinny and Mad."

"Oh yes?" said Aunt Augusta.

"Oh no . . ." groaned Dottie.

Aunty Lottie's idea was this: *to walk in a funny way.*

"If it makes you happy dear," said Aunt Augusta, smiling. "Now everyone do as I say. Keep your eyes open and your mouths shut and learn, learn, learn, because . . . WE'RE GOING ON AN AUNTY OUTING! First stop, Bobsy McBobsy's Fast Food Restaurant!"

With that, everyone rushed off behind Aunt Augusta towards the flashing cardboard sign.

As they entered, they got quite a shock.

"Oh no . . . it's a Bob dressed up as a fast food clown!" wailed Dottie. "How cheapo can you get!"

"Slack City!" muttered Joe.

"Now, before we sit down," began Aunt Augusta, "part of an aunty's job is to feed up these chilliwinks. Their parents rarely give them enough and it's usually only yucky healthy food. SO . . . what do we say when they tell us they've eaten enough?"

Aunty Flo answered immediately.

"Nonsense, have some more; there's no such thing as enough!"

"Good Aunty Flo . . . and altogether."

"Good . . . And off we go!"

They ate a lot of hamburgers.

Slurped a lot of milkshakes . . . and played with a lot of activity packs.

As soon as the very last crumb had left the very last plate, Aunt Augusta was at the door.

"Come on, let's get going; there's plenty more to see and do on an aunty outing."

Everyone bundled towards her.

"But, before we go, we have an important question to ask those nieces and neffys, don't we?"

Aunty Flo nodded wisely.

"We have to ask them if they need to go for

a WEE WEE, or in the case of our delightful
Skinny and Mad . . . a WOO WOO?"

"A WOO WOO?" murmured the confused
Aunty Lottie.

"A WOO blummin' WOO!" snapped Lottie,
jabbing her aunty with a finger.

"Got that?
Right then,
next stop
The Bobsy Museum!"

The little crowd followed Aunt Augusta down
the cardboard street.

"Now Aunties, on an Aunty Outing you must
never let a moment pass without being entertain-
ing, so while you're walking along you must play
one of those lovely games like, 'I'm Going On

100

A Picnic.' So, I'M going on a picnic and I'm going to take . . ."

My Camera!

My Notes

Lots of Money

An Aardvark

Some Iron Filings

A cheesy snack

My Swiss Army Penknife

A Cattle Prod

My New Aunties

"GOOD. Wasn't that fun? Oh look, here we are at the museum and in we go. Just follow me."

Once again they found themselves on another one of Aunt Augusta's whirlwind tours.

They scrambled past sarcophagi.

Goodness knows what these musty old things are, so just say the occasional "That's nice" or "Oooh look at that."

They scuttled past skeletons.

Look at these poor souls, they couldn't have had REAL aunties. Don't forget to keep pointing …

And skipped past stuffed animals (all cardboard of course).

Unless it's one of those "hands on" type exhibitions. Then you'll have to say all the same sorts of things, but jiggle everything about at the same time – got that?

And in no time at all it was time for lunch. Aunt Augusta herded everyone up to the cardboard canteen. As they got inside, a familiar figure appeared.

THERE'S A DIFFERENCE AT Mc BOBSY'S!

JOLLY HAT!

FUN PACK

Then it was time for MORE activity packs, MORE hamburgers and MORE milk shakes.

Hey! I'm getting a tummy like a Bob!

"Good girl. And, Aunties, what do we say to those nieces and neffys now we've finished?"
Everyone spoke at once, which is actually quite difficult to write down, *so* try and imagine all

103

these things being said at the same time:

Aunty Flo: "Would you like a wee wee?"

Aunty Gertie: "Would you like to powder your noseypoo?"

Aunty Prin: "Would you like to go to the horrible draughty old smelly toilet?"

Aunty Min: "Would you like a pound of cheddar?"

Aunty Lottie: "Would you like a wee woo?"

"GOOD!" smiled Aunt Augusta herding everyone into the street. "Now, let's get going. What game shall we play now? . . . Aunty Min?"

"Hide-and-seek?" squeaked Aunty Min.

"HIDE-AND-SEEK? What an unbelievably stupid thing to say! HOW can we play Hide-and-seek while we're walking along the road? . . . Aunty Gertie?"

"How about, Boot-the-swot-up-the-bot?" suggested Aunty Gertie, smirking across at Aunty Flo.

"I'd rather play Beat-the-cheat-on-the-seat?" retorted Aunty Flo, smirking across at Aunty Gertie.

It was then that a very embarrassing incident occurred and Joe took the following picture.

The two aunties involved had a gold star each taken away and the course was resumed as soon as they'd both written, "I must not act like a two-year-old" one hundred times.

"So, now that little hiccup has been sorted out, here we are at the theatre. Let's see what's on." said Aunt Augusta.

Everyone scrambled into a row of seats facing a pair of cardboard curtains.

"Um, as I'm not actually walking about here," began Aunty Lottie, "shall I just SIT in a funny way?"

"Yes dear," smiled Aunt Augusta, "you do that."

After a few moments the cardboard curtains swung open and on danced the Bobs dressed as vegetables.

Uh how simply marvellous! It's all about vegetables coming to life and dancing about.

During the interval, Aunt Augusta handed everyone a giant box of popcorn.

"I think I've eaten enough," groaned Aggie.

"Don't eat it if you don't want to niece," whispered Aunty Prin.

"I hope I didn't hear what I think I heard!" snapped Aunt Augusta. "That's not what we say, is it Aunty Prin? We say, 'Nonsense, have some more, there's no such thing as enough!' How will this poor child ever look loved by you if you don't feed her. Look at her, poor skinny thing. These little darlings have to eat as much as we can give them or they'll never be like my Bobs."

The show started again and, Aunt Augusta bent across and whispered softly to the aunties, "Children's shows are nearly always like this, terribly dreary. I find it a marvellous opportunity to have a quick snooze so you can wake up nice and refreshed when it's all over. Got that?"

... send in the cauliflowers ...

The Bobs sang. The Bobs danced. The Bobs fell over.

And in no time at all, the curtains swung shut and Aunt Augusta sprang to her feet.

"Show's over and off we all go."

"Isn't anyone going to ask if anyone wants a wee wee?" wailed Bertie.

"Afraid there's no time for that, and out we go for a final snackeroo and a lovely chit, chat, choo. And where better to go than . . ."

107

They ate and they chatted and they slurped and they played and just as they were all about to burst, Aunt Augusta stood up and announced that, "The Aunty Outing is over! You all did very well indeed but how can you tell if your niece or neffy's had a good time?"

Aunty Flo answered immediately, "Green face, fat tummy and lots of lovely groaning."

"Good! Aunty Flo, and we can measure which child has had the best outing by means of a Fat Gauge, a Groan Gauge and a Green Gauge. Bobs gauge them please."

"And the child who's had the best outing of all," chorused the Bobs, "is . . . Dottie!"

"That can't be right," sniped Dottie. "That dimmo couldn't possibly have done something properly!"

Aggie had an awful feeling that if she looked across at Aunty Prin, her hand would be up in the air.

She was absolutely correct.

"Excuse me," came the familiar voice.

Aunt Augusta looked slowly round.

The expression on her face would have made the Wicked Witch of the West decide to throw in her broomstick and take up flower arranging instead.

and as you can see ...
this tasteful arrangement

Aggie covered her eyes.
Joe zoomed in for a
close-up.

Don't you think
all that sweet sickly food
and rushing about is
terribly unhealthy for our
nieces and nephews?

Aunt Augusta blinked twice and then looked
away. "I didn't hear that did I?" she smiled
forcefully. "Those words did not enter my ears."

"I think she needs a hearing aid Min," muttered Aunty Prin.

Aggie looked at Aunty Prin. She wanted to
say,

Why do you keep doing this?
You said you'd try to be better
aunties for me, but
all you do is to keep
asking those horrible
questions and
making me
look stupid!

but because she was such a polite girl, she couldn't bring herself to say such a thing, but Aunty Prin must have sensed that she was feeling upset.

"I'm sorry niece," she began in the sort of voice that people use when they're not sorry at all, "but that silly fat woman talks such rubbish."

"But she's an expert," said Aggie very softly.

Aunty Prin looked away and decided very quietly to herself that she wouldn't ask any more questions. After all . . . they had *promised*.

We'll try and do this aunty course of yours. You're the only one who comes and visits us, and if you stopped coming, we'd probably never see anyone again.

"Now!" shrieked Aunt Augusta, looking suddenly very excited. "Our course is nearly over. Only one more step to complete and utter Auntiness. You have learned to kiss like an aunty, make woollies like an aunty, take an outing like an aunty; now you must learn how to *look* like an Aunty; so follow me!"

With that, she turned on her heel and headed back towards the Academy, not even mentioning that the Bobs were about to entertain everyone with some of their marvellous Viennese Whirl Ventriloquism. The little crowd followed.

CHAPTER NINE

Colanders & Conversations

When they arrived back upstairs, they found that the Knatty Knitters had gone and in their place were four frilly pink dressing tables.

As you can see, Aunty Lottie's was slightly different from the others.

Aggie sat down at her desk with her chin on her hands and felt really fed up. Her vision of the aunties accepting the Golden Knick-Knack was now little more than a faint blur.

Bertie's voice suddenly interrupted the blur.

"So how do you think yours are doing?" it said.

"Oh fine," said Aggie. "I mean they're not doing so well HERE but they'll probably practise all this when they get home." She then smiled feebly and wondered why she'd just told another PORKY.

"Mine won't," came Dottie's sneering voice. "I never realized what a complete thickie mine was. That 'walking in a funny way' was dreadful. It didn't make me laugh once."

"Oh come on," said Joe, joining the two other children at Aggie's desk, "your aunty did the coolest outing, and that walking she did was Fun City; it's going to be the highlight of my TV show."

"Well then, your SHOW is going to be even more boring than I first thought!" With that Dottie strode across to her aunty to give her another lecture about paying attention.

Now, while this conversation was going on, a totally different conversation was going on between Aunty Gertie and Aunt Augusta. This conversation was much quieter than the other one because . . . it was supposed to be secret.

But, if you'd have got quite close and listened very carefully, you would have heard this:

Aunty Gertie: *Mumble mumble mumble* **you could do with an extension** *mumble mumble* **more teachers** *mumble* **complete re-furbish-ment** mumble **lots more knick-knacks.**

Aunt Augusta: *Mumble mumble* **no money** *mumble.*

Aunty Gertie: *Mumble mumble* **could give you lots of money** *mumble mumble* **Golden Knick Knackypoo** *mumble* **for me** *mumblepoo.*

Then there was the sound of a lot of money being handed from one person to the other and slipped into a very colourful pocket.

Aunty Gertie then returned to her seat and Aunt Augusta walked to the front of the dressing tables and clapped her hands to get everyone's attention.

Well, my lovely aunties, we're nearly finished – just one more cherry, and the trifle of Aunty Perfection is complete!

At the mention of the word "trifle", both the Bob's mouths started watering like garden sprinklers.

"So there is still a chance for you slackers to catch up." Aunt Augusta flicked her eyes briefly in the direction of Aunty Prin and Aunty Min. "Now, this is perhaps the most condensed section of our course so far and will immediately be followed by our marvellous presentation ceremony, which I'm sure will be an occasion you'll never forget. So let's get on. Who can tell me what it is that makes a real aunty *look* like a real aunty? . . . Aunty Flo?"

"Colour," said Aunty Flo, smiling up from her notes, which she had chained to her desk.

"Absolutely. You certainly aren't a slacker are you Aunty Flo?" Aunty Flo shook her head and beamed smugly across at Aunty Gertie who immediately beamed smugly back.

Aunt Augusta continued, "Now Bobs, hold up our demonstration picture of the perfect aunty make-up."

The picture was very highly coloured. So highly coloured, in fact, that both Aunty Prin and Aunty Min had to cover their eyes.

"So. Colour is our byword. On our hair, on our faces, on our jewellery and, of course, in our clothes. And why do you think this is, Aunty Min?"

117

This was it . . . Aunty Min's last chance to answer a question right. Aggie held her breath.

Because it keeps the flies away?

Aggie sighed deeply.

Her vision disappeared.

"Keeps the flies away?" boomed Aunt Augusta. "What a perfectly ridiculous thing to say. You REALLY should have been a 'Skinny and Mad', but it's too late now. Anyway, the reason, as every REAL aunty will know, is that we want to be REMEMBERED."

"She's calling ME Skinny and Mad now, Prin," muttered Aunty Min.

Aunty Prin's eyes narrowed.

Aunt Augusta continued. "You know, I had lots and lots of aunties, but the only one I remember is my lovely Aunt Augusta. The rest just merge into one great grey globulation."

"And that's because, not only were none of them soft, sweet and sloppy, but they all used to have drab boring faces and wear drab boring clothes; rather like the sort you see in that dreadful B. Boring & Co. Catalogue. So ladies, to your dressing tables, and let the transformation commence!"

The aunties sat down on the padded seats. On the dressing tables in front of them were three boxes.

"Now don't you worry if you get into trouble, our experts will be on hand to help you."

"Would those *experts* be called Bob by any chancypoo?" asked Aunty Gertie.

"Why yes," trilled Aunt Augusta.

"Well, I'm sorry, but I only allow my face to be touched by *real* experts."

"NOT experts in Advanced Auntiness I'm sure; but you do whatever you find comfortable Aunty Gertie."

I certainly will Aunt Augusta.

"Now where's our lovely potty Aunty Lottie?"

Aunty Lottie looked up from amidst the garden gnomes.

120

"Your make-up dear, will be much the same as everyone else's, but remember this; your clothes will always come from jumble sales and smell of mothballs and instead of a lovely aunty hairstyle, you wear 'things on your head'. You know, like lampshades and cardboard boxes."

"Lampshades and cardboard boxes?" murmured Aunty Lottie.

"YES, LAMPSHADES AND CARDBOARD BOXES!" yelled Dottie, tutting so loudly her glasses jumped about six inches.

"SO! Ready to open up your boxes marked make-up, and . . . off we go!"

The children watched anxiously.

This is what was inside the boxes:

"Now, on with that make-up!"

Eyelids, eyelashes, lips, cheeks,
and finally . . . powder!

"Good! And on to those jingle janglys."

Bracelets, ear-rings, necklaces, and brooches.

"Good! And, finally . . . our marvellous Aunty Wigs!"

Why am I wearing a colander on my head?

Aunty Gertie, Aunty Flo, Aunty Prin, Aunty Min, Aunty Lottie.

"And that's it . . . our finished aunties! Now get up and give us all a little twirl. Don't they look something?"

The children's eyes and Joe's camera flicked along the line. They stood silently, staring in amazement.

Aggie looked at her aunties and was very relieved to see that they looked just as much like REAL aunties as all the others.

"Now Bobs, bring over the Auntometers for our final result. These little do-dads will tell us who is the most colourful and therefore the most Auntylike."

The Bobs pointed the Auntometers at the finished aunties.

The dials flickered and the pointers swayed and after a few seconds, came the Bob's chorus.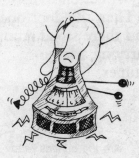

"The most colourful aunty of all is . . . Aunty Gertie!"

"Oh, how marvellous!" beamed Aunt Augusta. "Well done."

"Thank you," smiled Aunty Gertie.

Aggie looked nervously across at Aunty Prin and was quite surprised to see that she didn't have her hand up.

Perhaps there was some hope after all, she thought. At least they might get a diploma.

Suddenly, from just outside the door, there was a fanfare of trumpets.

Aunt Augusta's eyes lit up like fairy lights. "Ah, the time has come my sweet ones."

Then the door opened and there stood Aunty Joan carrying a large banner.

> Are the aunties ready to proceed to the Hall of Utter Auntiness?

"Yea the aunties are ready to proceed to the Hall of Utter Auntiness," replied Aunt Augusta in a very peculiar voice.

"Are they to the best of your knowledge, soft, sweet and sloppy?"

"Yea, they are to the best of my knowledge, soft, sweet and sloppy."

"Well, then," announced the smiling Aunty Joan, "let the Presentation Ceremony commence!"

The trumpets blew once more and the Bobs marched solemnly across the room. (Well, as solemnly as two such flibbily, flabbily, flollopy things can march across a room) and Aunt Augusta led the newly auntified party into the corridor.

"Follow me," she instructed with a smile and stepped in behind Aunty Joan. "The Golden Knick-Knack awaits."

"It certainly does," muttered Aunty Gertie. "It certainly does."

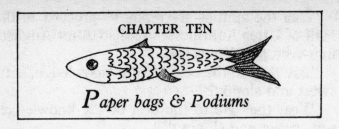

CHAPTER TEN

*P*aper bags & Podiums

On the short journey to the Hall of Utter Aunt-iness, Aunt Augusta, Aunty Joan and the Bobs sang a little song. It was probably an age-old Aunty chant handed on through generations of Aunty Academies. Either that or they were making it up as they went along, but whichever it was . . . this is how it went:

Knick-knack knick-knack knick-knack noo,
Aunties do what aunties do,
Knick-knack knick-knack knick-knack noppy,
Aunties are soft and sweet and sloppy . . .
(This was repeated about three times)

As often happens in musicals, while they were singing this, Aunty Flo (looking across at Aunty Gertie) began to sing this:

> *I'm sure to get the knick-knack . . .*
> *neh neh neh neh neh neh . . .*
> *I'm sure to get the knick-knack . . .*
> *neh neh neh . . .*

And while Aunty Flo was singing that, Aunty Gertie was singing this:

> *Don't be too sure . . . cockypants . . .*
> *Don't be so smuggypoo . . .*

And Aunty Lottie sang this:

> *Skinny and Mad . . . I want to be*
> *Skinny and Mad!*

And Aunty Prin and Aunty Min sang this:

> *Iron filings . . . why couldn't we have seen*
> *some iron filings . . .*

It all built up into one great glorious crescendo which ground to a joyous halt at the door of The Hall of Utter Auntiness.

Whereupon, Aunt Augusta marched inside and shut the door behind her.

The aunties waited nervously.

"Don't look so worried," smiled Aunty Joan. "You'll all get your diplomas . . . everyone always does."

"What about the Knick-Knack?" said Aunty Lottie who was shaking so much her bloomers were flapping.

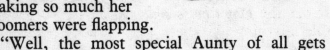

"Well, the most special Aunty of all gets that."

Both Aunty Gertie and Aunty Flo smiled.

Bertie noticed this and worried. He knew his aunty well enough to know when she was up to something.

"Do you think I said enough funny things?" muttered Aunty Lottie, blinking down at Dottie.

"No I don't. You hardly said any, and the ones you did say weren't even half funny. I bet you haven't won anything . . . unless there's a prize for the most pathetic Skinny and Mad who's ever been."

"Do you think WE'LL get the Golden Knick-Knack, Prin?" squeaked Aunty Min, looking up at her sister.

"I most certainly hope not!" snapped Aunty Prin. "I wouldn't want the horrible shiny thing."

"It would be nice to get a diploma though wouldn't it, I've never had anything like that before. We could put it on the mantelpiece, next to that iron filing you found."

"Mmm . . ." said Aunty Prin after a while.

> I suppose that would be rather nice ... it might be quite exciting!

It was the first time she'd said anything like that in the whole of her life.

Suddenly, the doors opened and there stood Aunt Augusta resplendent in her Robes of Presentation.

"Follow me." She smiled and led the little group into the Hall.

The Hall of Utter Auntiness was a very large room. At one end there was a small stage; in the middle of which, standing on a podium, was the Golden Knick-Knack.

The Knick-Knack was beautiful and shiny and quite useless.

Beside the podium stood a table and on this table was a basket which held the diplomas, all tied with pink ribbons.

As the party walked through the Hall, Aggie noticed two things in this order:

1. The worker aunts were sitting in the audience.
2. They all had paper bags over their heads.

It was Joe who asked the question that was on everyone's lips.

"Hey man. Why are their heads in Paper-bag City?"

"Because, young man," replied Aunt Augusta, beaming, "they must not see the 'improved' aunties approach. Otherwise we would not get the 'Worker Aunt Gasp' and the 'Worker Aunt Gasp' is one way of telling how well we've done. Right then children you sit down over there. Aunties, follow me up on to the stage."

The children filed into the front row. Aggie looked up at her aunties and suddenly felt some-

thing that really surprised her. She felt proud.
Despite all Aunty Prin's interruptions and Aunty
Min's silly answers they had tried their best, and
that's what REALLY counted.

Aunt Augusta walked across to the podium
and the aunties stood in a little line behind her.

At the back of the hall stood the Bobs.

"Worker aunts," she intoned with a smile.
"Can you hear me?"

There was a lot of rustling as all the paper
bags nodded.

"Good. The aunties are here, awaiting your
reaction, so remove your bags . . . NOW!"

The worker aunts took their bags off and all
of a sudden there was a gasp so great, Aggie
could feel her hair being sucked up behind her.

"My goodness!" boomed Aunt Augusta.
"What a gasp that was . . . do we have a Gaspometer reading my Bobs?"

"Yes Aunty . . . it's 95!"

"Splendid. A very good gasp indeed, and now let us move on. The time has come to present you with our marvellous diplomas!"

There was a mass muttering. The children looked excitedly at one another.

"The first is for a truly remarkable Skinny and Mad aunty, who excelled at her outings. I'm talking, of course, about potty Aunty Lottie!"

Aunty Lottie shrieked with delight and scuttled forwards to accept her diploma.

Everyone applauded.

MMM ... thank you I'm sure I didn't deserve this.

I'll say you didn't!

"And the next diploma is for someone who has been an example to us all and a perfect pleasure to teach. I'm referring of course to . . . Aunty Gertie!"

Aunty Flo's mouth fell open.

Bertie shifted uncomfortably in his seat. Everyone clapped politely. Aunty Gertie stepped forwards.

How marvellous I'm sooo thrill'dypoo!

"The next diploma is for someone who has done really quite well . . . Aunty Flo!"

"Really quite well?" thought Aunty Flo. "Three months' work and, 'really quite well!' "

Everyone clapped. Aunty Flo stepped forwards.

Thanks a bunch.

Still, if I'm getting the Knick-Knack then I don't suppose they'd overdo the diploma

Aggie bit her lip nervously.

"And now," began Aunt Augusta, "on to the Golden Knick-Knack. As you all may know . . ."

"Um . . . excuse me," came Aunty Prin's voice suddenly from behind Aunt Augusta.

"Yes?" snapped Aunt Augusta.

"Aunty Min and I didn't get a diploma."

Aunty Min shook her head.

"Well, you were both so supremely useless, neither of you deserved one."

Aggie clapped her hand to her mouth.

There was a rustling and muttering around the room.

"But Aunty Joan said . . ." began Aunty Min.

"I don't care WHAT Aunty Joan said! When I say no diplomas, I *mean* NO diplomas!"

Aunty Prin bit her lip.

"Oh, but I was forgetting," said Aunt Augusta smarmily, "you *do* get something."

Little Aunty Min's eyes lit up.

"Two dunce's hats. Put them on for them please Aunty Joan. Anyway, as I was saying . . ."

Aggie was dumbstruck. She watched in complete disbelief as Aunty Joan placed the hats on her aunties' heads.

There we are.

Aunt Augusta continued beaming away at the audience.

"So . . . the winner of this week's Golden Knick-Knack is . . ."

Aunty Flo got ready to step forwards.

Joe zoomed in on her.

"Aunty . . . Gertie!"

"WHAT?" exclaimed Aunty Flo. "But she didn't get one question right. AND she cheated!"

"Unfair City!" exclaimed Joe.

"Please Aunty Flo. Real aunties MUST be good losers; now please calm down."

Aunty Gertie strode forwards and accepted the Knick-Knack with a knowing wink.

Aunt Augusta, sensing that things were getting a little uneasy, decided to forge ahead and get the ceremony over with as quickly as possible.

"Now, it's time for our passing-out parade and what better way to start a parade than with a rousing, aunty party piece. So, my beautiful Bobs, let us see the words."

The Bobs held up a large song sheet.

"Now Aunties, let's all sing the song and make your nieces and nephews proud."

The aunties began to sing. The worker aunts clapped along and Aunt Augusta's voice soared above them all.

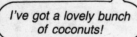

136

"Now, don't forget to point your finger. Look your nieces and nephews in the eye as you sing, 'big ones small ones, some as big as *your* head'."

Aunt Augusta danced up and down the little line singing and smiling and waving her arms around.

Aggie could barely bring herself to look at the aunties but when she did she saw something that just about broke her heart. They were shuffling from side to side in their pointy dunce's hats trying to sing the song, and Aggie knew that they were doing it for her.

But sadder still, when she looked a little closer, she could see that little Aunty Min was crying.

Then something happened.

Aggie began to feel very cross, very cross indeed, crosser than she had ever felt before. And all this crossness was pushing away her good manners, her niceness, her politeness, and, suddenly, she was jumping to her feet and shouting in the loudest voice possible.

STOP!
STOP THIS NOW!

The expression on her face would have sent the charging rhinoceros, the creature-who-slurped-from-the-Black-Lagoon, AND the Wicked Witch of the West scuttling off behind the nearest sofa.

There was a crash from the back of the room as the Bobs dropped their song sheet in fright, and ran from the room blubbering. Up on the stage, the aunties had all stopped mid-prance, and now stood as still as statues. The only one who seemed to be moving was Aunt Augusta who looked round slowly and menacingly, her eyes fixing on Aggie in a terrifying snarl – the sight of which caused several Worker Aunts to put their bags back over their heads.

Aggie took a deep breath. Joe zoomed in on her face.

"This is completely unfair," she shouted, "my aunties were no worse than any of the others. Why didn't they get a diploma?"

"Because," spat Aunt Augusta, "a diploma tells the world that you're a REAL aunty; and pigs will fly before those sorry specimens become REAL aunties."

Well, that's good! Because if being a REAL aunty means that they have to wear horrible clothes and make-up and say stupid things all the time and knit me disgusting sweaters and stuff me full of so much food that I go green, then I don't want any REAL aunties ... I want the ones I had before!

The worker aunts gasped. (A gasp which, incidentally, registered an awful lot higher than 95 on the Gaspometer.)

Aggie then turned and faced the children.

"Come on, be honest. Do you lot really want to end up looking like the Bobs? 'Cos that's what would happen if you had an aunty like Aunt Augusta. You'd ALL have brown fairy kisses on your teeth and tummies full of love. Tummies full of fat more like. And do you really think that your aunties look NICE? Look at them! Would you REALLY feel happy walking down the street with someone who looked like that?"

The children looked up.

Bertie bit his lip.

"Well I would," squeaked Dottie. "I think they look lovely."

"Well, YOU wear this lot then!" yelled Aunty Lottie, removing the colander from her head and beginning to climb out of her bloomers. "YOU be Skinny and Mad!" and with that she threw the whole lot down on Dottie's head.

Dottie's mouth shut as if pulled by a drawstring.

"This is outrageous!" bellowed Aunt Augusta. "How dare you cock a snook at my methods!"

"But Aggie's right!" boomed Aunty Gertie. "We do look embarrassing. I don't want this dreadful Golden Knick-Knackypoo. You can forget your extension. Give me back the extra money I slipped you!"

"EXTRA MONEY!" everyone yelled in horror.

They all looked at Aunt Augusta, who suddenly looked very guilty.

"I knew it!" yelped Aunty Flo. "I thought something was going on, you little cheater!"

And with that, she and Aunty Gertie started fighting again.

And what about
OUR money!

yelled Aggie.

"I don't know about everyone
else but I'm demanding my
'piggybank-money-back guarantee'!"

"Me too!" said Bertie. "I really don't see why
I should spend my hard-saved piggybank money
on that old cheatypoo!"

"So am I," beamed Joe. "I can use the money
to finish my TV show!"

All the children turned and faced Dottie.

"You blummin' better too!" warned Aunty
Lottie. "You borrowed it off me in the first place
remember!"

"Oh, all right then, so will I," snapped Dottie,
trying hard to avoid her Aunty's jabbing finger.

"This is REALLY most irregular," spluttered
Aunty Joan, and then loads of things seemed to
happen at the same time. Things like this:

Aunty Lottie chased Dottie with her 'jabbing finger'.

And this:

The worker aunts tried to sweep everyone up!

And indeed this:

Joe and Bertie tried to pull their battling aunties apart.

142

Aggie looked up at her two Aunties.

"I'm sorry . . ." she said, "REALLY I am."

Auntie Prin looked sternly down from the stage . . . then suddenly her face broke into a wide grin. "What's there to be sorry about?" she smiled. "It's the best fun we've had in ages!"

"REALLY?" said Aggie.

"Really," squeaked Auntie Min. "It was much better than cleaning the door knob."

All around them the room was in uproar, and in the midst of it all . . . stood Aunt Augusta wringing her hands in spectacular despair.

"Never," she wailed.
"Never, in all my years
training aunties has such
a thing ever happened.
And to hear a child speaking
to an adult in such a way!"
Aunty Joan patted her arm reassuringly.

"It's typical of children today, Madam. They don't know what's good for them!"

Aggie heard this and looked up.

"Well, you see that's where you're wrong," she said. "Things have changed since the days of Aunt Augusta the First. Children today DO know what's good for them. I mean, we all LIKE sicky food but we now know that too much is bad for us. Look, if you REALLY love those two blobs, you'll put them on a diet and take them off to see a dentist."

Then Aggie said goodbye to Joe, Bertie and Dottie.

and then turned and marched away. Down the corridors, through the reception (pausing briefly to pick up her piggybank), out of the door and all the way back to the aunties' house.

"Goodbye then," said Aggie, smiling as Aunty Prin and Aunty Min disappeared behind the Sludge Grey door once more. Just as she was about to walk away Aunty Prin spoke.

"Are you coming to tea tomorrow?" she said.

Aggie turned and looked back. "If you want me to!"

"Yes we do niece. We DO want you to, don't we Min?"

Aunty Min nodded.

"All right," said Aggie with a wave. "See you then."

Sardines & Sundays

The next day Aggie went to tea at her aunties' house. She arrived promptly at 2 o'clock just as she always did and sat down in the armchair in the front room.

The two aunties were sitting where they always sat, side-by-side on the raggedy sofa watching the TV.

146

The programme they were watching was about the similarity of cheese and iron filings.

At 3 o'clock Aunty Prin spoke.

Tea-time,

she said. And then she added, smiling ever so slightly,

special tea-time.

Whereupon Aunty Min produced
a plate that was covered
by a pretty paper doily.

*Help yourself
to a sardine ...
sandwich,*

she said, lifting up the paper doily. There, sure
enough, was a plate of lovely sardine *sandwiches*.

Thank you

said Aggie and tucked in.

At 4 o'clock the doorbell rang and it was Aggie's
mum who had come to take her home.

"Goodbye," said Aggie, "and thanks for the
sardine . . . sandwich."

THE
END

Other great reads *from* **Red Fox**

Further Red Fox titles that you might enjoy reading are listed on the following pages. They are available in bookshops or they can be ordered directly from us.

If you would like to order books, please send this form and the money due to:

ARROW BOOKS, BOOKSERVICE BY POST, PO BOX 29, DOUGLAS, ISLE OF MAN, BRITISH ISLES. Please enclose a cheque or postal order made out to Arrow Books Ltd for the amount due, plus 30p per book for postage and packing to a maximum of £3.00, both for orders within the UK. For customers outside the UK, please allow 35p per book.

NAME _____

ADDRESS _____

_____

Please print clearly.

Whilst every effort is made to keep prices low, it is sometimes necessary to increase cover prices at short notice. If you are ordering books by post, to save delay it is advisable to phone to confirm the correct price. The number to ring is THE SALES DEPARTMENT 071 (if outside London) 973 9700.

THE SNIFF STORIES Ian Whybrow

Things just keep happening to Ben Moore. It's dead hard avoiding disaster when you've got to keep your street cred with your mates *and* cope with a family of oddballs at the same time. There's his appalling 2½ year old sister, his scatty parents who are into healthy eating and animal rights and, worse than all of these, there's Sniff! If only Ben could just get on with his scientific experiments and his attempt at a world beating *Swampbeast* score . . . but there's no chance of that while chaos is just around the corner.

ISBN 0 09 975040 6   £2.99

J.B. SUPERSLEUTH Joan Davenport

James Bond is a small thirteen-year-old with spots and spectacles. But with a name like that, how can he help being a supersleuth?

It all started when James and 'Polly' (Paul) Perkins spotted a teacher's stolen car. After that, more and more mysteries needed solving. With the case of the Arabian prince, the Murdered Model, the Bonfire Night Murder and the Lost Umbrella, JB's reputation at Moorside Comprehensive soars.

But some of the cases aren't quite what they seem . . .

ISBN 0 09 971780 8   £2.99

Other great reads *from* **Red Fox**

THE WINTER VISITOR   Joan Lingard

Strangers didn't come to Nick Murray's home town in winter. And they didn't lodge at his house. But Ed Black had—and Nick Murray didn't like it.

Why had Ed come? The small Scottish seaside resort was bleak, cold and grey at that time of year. The answer, Nick begins to suspect, lies with his mother—was there some past connection between her and Ed?

ISBN 0 09 938590 2   £1.99

STRANGERS IN THE HOUSE   Joan Lingard

Calum resents his mother remarrying. He doesn't want to move to a flat in Edinburgh with a new father and a thirteen-year-old stepsister. Stella, too, dreads the new marriage. Used to living alone with her father she loathes the idea of sharing their small flat.

Stella's and Calum's struggles to adapt to a new life, while trying to cope with the problems of growing up are related with great poignancy in a book which will be enjoyed by all older readers.

ISBN 0 09 955020 2   £2.99

Discover the great animal stories of Colin Dann

JUST NUFFIN

The Summer holidays loomed ahead with nothing to look forward to except one dreary week in a caravan with only Mum and Dad for company. Roger was sure he'd be bored.

But then Dad finds Nuffin: an abandoned puppy who's more a bundle of skin and bones than a dog. Roger's holiday is transformed and he and Nuffin are inseparable. But Dad is adamant that Nuffin must find a new home. Is there *any* way Roger can persuade him to change his mind?

ISBN 0 09 966900 5   £2.99

KING OF THE VAGABONDS

'You're very young,' Sammy's mother said, 'so heed my advice. Don't go into Quartermile Field.'

His mother and sister are happily domesticated but Sammy, the tabby cat, feels different. They are content with their lot, never wondering what lies beyond their immediate surroundings. But Sammy is burningly curious and his life seems full of mysteries. Who is his father? Where has he gone? And what is the mystery of Quartermile Field?

ISBN 0 09 957190 0   £2.99

Other great reads *from* **Red Fox**

The Millennium books are novels for older readers from the very best science fiction and fantasy writers

A DARK TRAVELLING   Roger Zelazny

An 'ordinary' 14-year-old, James Wiley has lost his father to a parallel world in the darkbands. With the help of his sister Becky, James, the exchange student and Uncle George, the werewolf, James goes in search of his parent.

ISBN 0 09 960970 3   £2.99

PROJECT PENDULUM   Robert Silverberg

Identical twins Sean and Eric have been chosen for a daring experiment. One of them will travel into the distant past. The other into the distant future. And with each swing of the time pendulum they will be further apart . . .

ISBN 0 09 962460 5   £2.99

THE LEGACY OF LEHR   Katherine Kurtz

The interstellar cruiser *Valkyrie* is forced to pick up four sinister, exotic cats, much to the captain's misgivings. His doubts appear justified when a spate of vicious murders appear on board.

ISBN 0 09 960960 6   £2.99

CHESS WITH A DRAGON   David Gerrold

The Galactic InterChange was the greatest discovery in history . . . but now it had brought disaster. Unless Yake could negotiate a deal with the alien in front of him, mankind would be reduced to a race of slaves.

ISBN 0 09 960950 9   £2.99

Other great reads ❦ *from* **Red Fox**

**The latest and funniest joke books are from
Red Fox!**

THE OZONE FRIENDLY JOKE BOOK
Kim Harris, Chris Langham, Robert Lee,
Richard Turner

What's green and highly dangerous?
How do you start a row between conservationists?
What's green and can't be rubbed out?

Green jokes for green people (non-greens will be pea-green
when they see how hard you're laughing), bags and bags of them
(biodegradable of course).

All the jokes in this book are printed on environmentally
friendly paper and every copy you buy will help GREENPEACE
save our planet.

* David Bellamy with a machine gun.
* Pour oil on troubled waters.
* The Indelible hulk.

ISBN 0 09 973190 8 £1.99

THE HAUNTED HOUSE JOKE BOOK
John Hegarty

There are skeletons in the scullery . . .
Beasties in the bath . . .
There are spooks in the sitting room
And jokes to make you laugh . . .

Search your home and see if we are right. Then come back,
sit down and shudder to the hauntingly funny and eerily rib-
rattling jokes in this book.

ISBN 0 09 9621509 £1.99

Other great reads ✒ *from* **Red Fox**

Haunting fiction for older readers from Red Fox

THE XANADU MANUSCRIPT
John Rowe Townsend

There is nothing unusual about visitors in Cambridge.

So what is it about three tall strangers which fills John with a mixture of curiosity and unease? Not only are they strikingly handsome but, for apparently educated people, they are oddly surprised and excited by normal, everyday events. And, as John pursues them, their mystery only seems to deepen.

Set against a background of an old university town, this powerfully compelling story is both utterly fantastic and oddly convincing.

'An author from whom much is expected and received.' *Economist*

ISBN 0 09 975180 1 £2.99

ONLOOKER Roger Davenport

Peter has always enjoyed being in Culver Wood, and dismissed the tales of hauntings, witchcraft and superstitions associated with it. But when he starts having extraordinary visions that are somehow connected with the wood, and which become more real to him than his everyday life, he realizes that something is taking control of his mind in an inexplicable and frightening way.

Through his uneasy relationship with Isobel and her father, a Professor of Archaeology interested in excavating Culver Wood, Peter is led to the discovery of the wood's secret and his own terrifying part in it.

ISBN 0 09 975070 8 £2.99

Other great reads from **Red Fox**

AMAZING ORIGAMI FOR CHILDREN
Steve and Megumi Biddle

Origami is an exciting and easy way to make toys, decorations and all kinds of useful things from folded paper.

Use leftover gift paper to make a party hat and a fancy box. Or create a colourful lorry, a pretty rose and a zoo full of origami animals. There are over 50 fun projects in Amazing Origami.

Following Steve and Megumi's step-by-step instructions and clear drawings, you'll amaze your friends and family with your magical paper creations.

ISBN 0 09 966180 2   £5.99

MAGICAL STRING   Steve and Megumi Biddle

With only a loop of string you can make all kinds of shapes, puzzles and games. Steve and Megumi Biddle provide all the instructions and diagrams that are needed to create their amazing string magic in another of their inventive and absorbing books.

ISBN 0 09 964470 3   £2.50